TRANSLUCENT VACANT HEAD

MARIA OLON TSAROUCHA

Translucent Vacant Head

Published in the United States of America
ISBN 979-8-9926877-3-6 (paperback)
ISBN: 979-8-9926877-4-3 (kindle)
Supraconscious You
150 Bogert St, Totowa, NJ 07512
info@supraconscious.co

Order Information and Rights Permission:
For Book Rights Adaptation and other Rights Permission send us an email at info@supraconscious.co

First published in Greece in 2011 by Heridanos Publishing House. The English edition published in 2025 by Supraconscious You. Translation by Konstantine Matsoukas.

Translucent Vacant Head

*stored memory is barbed memory. The memory which is free
to fly like a bird outside the mind is childhood memory*

*I choose the latter memory to record the experience and the
former I choose to lay charges*

*to Konstantine, Elia
and melia*

this

this book is a tapestry
of fragmented memories
drifting through untitled pages
weaving the fleeting whispers
of identity's discovery

this is a story told through
fabrications for otherwise
it cannot be told

the condition

In my books there is no biographical note, and I sign with an alias. That's probably because I happen to believe that the real Chris has nothing in common with Chris the writer and, as a result, I am always absent even when I am present at some place.

That's probably because as a child, my parents told me I had a twin sister who died at birth. On the basis of scientific explanation to do with the psychology of twins, every time I experienced loss as such, and absence as presence, a part of myself died with her and a part of her lives in me.

That's probably because the loss I suffered from age naught, marked me a lot more than the baleful family secret itself of my sister's death, which my parents did not disclose. A secret that surfaced like a dead fish floating in the fishbowl when, a few months before I started writing our auto mythography, our parents revealed to me that apart from being my sister's twin, we were also Siamese.

the hair-parting

When I was a child, we lived in an apartment on the south side of the city as it's seen on the map. In an empty house across the street for the duration of one cold winter and a hot summer, lived a child my age. x. was a scrawny, fatherless boy whose mother, a good-looking woman with red hair and accentuated bust, dressed him rain or shine in short trousers and patent leather shoes and she parted his honey-colored hair straight down the middle, all the way to the back of his head. x.'s hair-parting was impressive, it became the departure point of much musing. A feminine trail inscribed on a male child's head. That was the time when I started inscribing letters.

the writer

She has no form or shape when she makes her appearance, I don't know what color the orbs of her eyes are and whether her skin is coarse or smooth, but I do know she's there, she is occupying a compact, three-dimensional space and she's whispering "come, now, with, me".

Many times, I tried to seize her with my hands, so she would become the line of life on my palm. Other times I brag self-importantly without considering there might be something I have yet to invent about melia, sipping my orange-scented chamomile under the trees overhanging the yard, with the white-and-black dog next to me, my companion since childhood with his one eye white and the other one black.

Or, if I don't follow her, her face, which does not actually exist, evanesces and then I lose my sense of self and sink in loneliness, the only state of being which I think of as real. Until the next time melia touches me, tapping my shoulder with her finger three times, and I turn to see her and suddenly realize that it is melia that controls me and not I melia. I am well enough aware, so that I can have these thoughts without meriting punishment, that melia will soon leave me.

What can she possibly expect from me, really? I mete out justice to her with the aim of resurrecting the secret love I harbor for her. What more can I impart to this creature and what more does she wish for me to know that I don't already?

I need to wait a while longer, just a while longer, until she reaches her own country, the one she's been searching for all these years, away from her family home, just a while longer until she appears at the place where I live, to disclose her desire to me. Her journey has been long and tortuous and melia has managed the hardest thing of all, to not get lost in it.

the subject

I anticipate seeing the country. It'll take a while longer before I reach it. I do not know it, I sense it. My eyes full of wrinkles. My thoughts are migrating. My feet walk upon the sea. Its waters heal the itinerary of my life. The prow is deserted but for me. My very own country feels like my other half. I anticipate seeing the country. It won't take quite as long now.

I'll be arriving in a bit. No change to my posture. A squid inside the water ejects its ink and in my reflection I see a young child watching the fish swimming in the sea. I remember father's fish. I remember the day I left the family home, when the water of the aquarium was poisoned by their urine because I'd given them too much food. The young child from another time, in short trousers, shiny shoes and his hair well combed, has been sitting in the middle of the ship with his laughing eyes and watching me for hours.

I am not afraid.

That young child looks like me.
Time is getting less.

The country now is visible.

Beautiful country. Such beautiful country.

I go up to her. It is time she knew.

The ship touches the body of the only land that can contain me, and I set foot on its ground. The young child follows behind. He glances furtively at my lame leg. He doesn't wish me to see him looking. I smile a little resentfully but also with a sigh of relief. I can't remember what modesty has made me steal glances at my own lame leg, which has, nevertheless, lent me such support. I have tried to negotiate many times, but my leg has a way of its own of deciding on my course. My leg has been taking care of me since the day I was born.

My name is melia, gender feminine. In no document have my congenital defects been recorded "the girl's head is vacant, she has no brain", "the child has one leg different to the other", neonate reflexes normal, heart rate normal, appearance normal.

writer-subject relationship

melia's eyes looked up to confirm the temporary need for care.

There was nothing in the sky that signaled rainfall, there were only remnants of fear left in her. The sea was ever so quiet, its waves wiped out by a pencil eraser. While the ship crossed the erased sea, melia pondered: "how orphaned I have been from safety".

the meeting

My paradoxical first meeting with melia four years ago
will stay lodged in me forever. Despicable times. A miserly
survival. My sleep would last for days and nights, my eyes
had no way of opening. I was hiding in the dark under the
woolen blanket, had no appetite, my body and mind ossified.
My intestinal system was on strike. It had curled up close
to my sex and was aiding and abetting the inhuman, sly
catatonia against myself. Food was an obstruction and, so,
it was rejected. Sadness about my existence was weighing
me down, blatantly indifferent towards my person.

That freezing morning of December, I had arranged a
meeting with my publisher. I had no news for him. I'd run
out of ideas. All inspiration had dried up, my mind was
a punishing, wicked stepmother. The alarm clock started
to ring more and more loudly, a funereal toll inside the
chambers of my scull, in an attempt to persuade me to
save what of myself was still left. (I don't actually recall
ever buying an alarm clock, I forget).

The alarm clock went silent though I hadn't reached out
to it. I timidly pushed aside the woolen blanket, and it was
then that I saw her. She was sitting next to the bedside table

in my small room. I was startled by the implausibility of a feminine presence in my solitary space, but I wasn't afraid. On the bedside table she had placed a picture of herself and me embracing. There was slim chance of that being real, we hadn't even met, was the instantaneous thought, summoned by what presence of mind I still possessed.

She was smiling in a way of her own as if she had disclaimed her life and her memory. A need stronger than the relationship we were going to forge, was compelling her to speak and entrust her secret to me. I felt intimidated by the trust she was putting in me, yet I didn't pull back. melia was asking to tell the story of her life and I felt the need to commune with her words, not yet knowing that only through her words would I come to understand and accept my own fixation and dissolution, caused by Father's death and mother's abuse.

She then fell silent and served me a plate of food. She appraised me better than I did the many years in which I'd gone hungry. She was the only one I had left before even I had time to love her.

The food she offered me that first time was just enough for me to be sated. All the following mornings I would find her standing there by the bedside table in my small room, waiting for me to emerge out of my darkness.

In time, she set conditions for me; she asked me to be very careful with what I wanted to say in writing her story, since she herself hadn't been allowed any frivolity and was extremely methodical with her emotions, taking a long time to decide what she wanted before she acted.

She wondered how much she'd been allowed to be herself, with so many fragments floating inside her like itinerant land masses dislodged by an earthquake. How she wished to be in her own skin, she was no snake, she hadn't another one to change into. How she wished to speak in her own words, to line up in a row the letters of her own alphabet. She said that it had all been "difficult", the first word she'd heard through the walls of her mother's belly, "difficult" was what her father had said boldly, insolently, when he had been told the baby was a girl. And dad's "difficult" always took her back to her first embryonic memory.

It has all been "difficult" dad, and the most "difficult" thing of all is that no one may question your Word, melia often thought. She very much wanted for nothing to be "difficult" for me, yet I took secret notes which I hid in the lining of my read coat, convinced of their usefulness.

They teach us, do they not, how to live until such time as we can teach ourselves how to live through the obscure present intervening between life and death.

The secret notes became my own salvation. The more I surrendered to her, the more I came out of my darkness and discovered in her words a sliver of light.

My shadow faithfully followed me as melia accompanied me to the exit of my thinking. She would open it for me.

She knew I only ever came out of my own "difficult" when there was sun and, since where I lived, the sun wasn't going to turn up for a long while, I needed to take the step outside on my own. The outside was changed and as my foot hovered, I heard crackling sounds, the footsteps of imaginary beings from my life as it had been, which I'd left behind. I was forever glancing backwards to catch my shadow in melia and in the little boy staring into my eyes.

the birth

melia was growing inside her mom's belly like any normal child. An embryonic life with no external interference. Mom understood her, missed her, desired her, listened to her. The liver, the heart and the umbilical glands connected them, like abundant natural resources. They mutually fed into one other with the same assurance as that the sun is going to rise each and every morning.

In the nine months, her mom didn't tell her a single lie. Mom was still healthy. Outside her body the glass pane shattered, the cheese-pie burnt in the oven, the relatives were being anxious. Then, the terrible news got out. The embryo suffered from a malfunction. It had no brain.

melia's mother was not sure whether she should have this child, with everyone and everything assuring her that anything of the sort was impossible. The doctors knew it, her mother knew it, her father knew it, the girl didn't. She wanted to be born, and not the doctors, not mom, not dad would stand in her way.

One bright day on a straight highway, the car kept accelerating way past the speed limit. Her dad was the driver and sole passenger, thinking of the child and muttering to himself "difficult".

Months passed and melia was born. The doctors wondered what they ought to do. Mom and dad refused to let the girl become the subject of experiments. She was to stay in an incubator, for as long as she managed to breathe. Everything was happening mechanically, the doctors said, a brain outside the head cannot provide any orders. The head was empty. melia's head was empty.

Time passed and the empty head gave the lie to every prognosis. melia was going to have a normal life except for one handicap. She would limp.

mom

melia's mom never spoke again since the day of her birth. The first and last words that flew out of her mouth as soon as she set eyes on the girl, were "to give birth to a child, you must first exist"; she then sunk into silence withholding the truth of her utterances and leaving melia's dad guessing.

Every dawn she got up, washed the night shadows off her face, pinned her hair up with a clip, went down the steps to the icon of the Virgin Mary and lit the oil- lamp.

Prayer had become second nature to her after she had the child. She didn't want to be parted from it, yet she wished it were dead. Every day before the icon the same vision, the Virgin Mary walks into her son's grave and lights a candle before his image. She then remains standing for a while. In the recess below his image, in a breach of the moist wall, there is a vase with lilies and a glass of water. She picks up the glass and waters the lilies. She is aware that she is not his biological mother, she is aware that he is the child she has desired. She is aware that the body of her desire is dead. She is aware that the only relationship she may negotiate after his death is that o mourning and absence. She misses him. She mourns him. Across from her, his form enclosed in the familiar mantle, the one in which he was wrapped after his death, is calmly staring back at her.

melia's mom sat in the kitchen rocking chair. Her cheeks were blushing red with guilt as if she'd just committed fornication. With a dead woman's pallor, she was in the process of gutting the orange to eat it whole, including the peel. Every day she repeated the same procedure.

The young girl was observing her mom and being initiated into the act of repetition, was ingesting modes of behavior. Many times, when a spontaneous act of hers broke the rules that according to her parents, circumscribed the bounds of normal behavior, her dad's criticism, on the rare occasions when he was home and melia's need for his affirmation, caused her to get into strict animadversions with herself and to doubt even her original motive, the motive to live. Confusion set in her mind and this made her sad.

Why should mom be praying to the Virgin Mary if I'm fine? Is it that I shouldn't be thinking because I have no brain or is my lame leg to blame, melia often wondered.

Mom was praying, so, melia did too.

Mo[m]nster please

Mo[m]nster please don't
Mo[m]nster please don't come inside my mind and make me cry

Mo[m]nster please don't come into my dreams at night and scare me, I just want to sleep quietly, and I can't because of the sound of your terrible footsteps what terrible feet

what an enormous ugly body you have

and what large mousy ears to listen to me praying and take me to the wicked magic "land of mom and dad"
Mo[m]nster please don't call dad

I'll be good, I'll be the world's most normal child.

Mom had a brain and melia had a memory. And this was the unbreachable, unspoken agreement between the two women until mom stopped using her brain.

They teach us, do they not, how to live until we can teach ourselves how to live through the obscure present intervening between life and death.

Every time melia's mom sat at the kitchen rocking chair to gut oranges, she experienced the boundary of her death. The only thing distorting her perception about her life and death was the existence of the child she'd given birth to. She possessed no brain and, so, everybody thought she didn't think, everyone behaved as if melia had died at birth.

the code

My mom wore a huge pair of knickers.

They covered up what should be familiar territory to me. Nevertheless, for my part, I felt I was a wished-for miscarriage, a non-normal child that would send dad away from her.

My mom has no tongue.

Her tongue got twisted lots of times and it got tied up in knots like a snake that asphyxiates in order not to spill deadly poison, when her desire for me to be another miscarriage went unanswered. In her prayers, she had been asking god for miscarriages. Not even for dad to stop being so boundlessly fertile.

It was like I was been born out of mom's mouth. On a summer day, as she was eating watermelon and spitting out the pips, she spat me out as well. And dad was caught off guard. His first mental instruction was to throw me away. Until I squawked loudly so he could see the pip was a baby.

My mom's tongue was the umbilical cord that bound us together for the duration of a lifetime in which we had to submit to each other's presence. Since the day of my birth, my mom never spoke again.

She wrote me notes, every time she wanted to say something she wrote a note. I learned this way that the things which truly have a reason to be said, are few and far between. She sang lullabies, spoke to me about love, criticized me, through notes. She wrote them while dad was away.

The stronger the code between us became, the more my mom desired me until she even loved me. And the more she loved me the more she replaced me with dad. Dad had put me on probation. I had to satisfy his wish for an unnatural maleness in my person. Only thus would he accept me. He never did accept me. I never did become a boy. I was born a girl. Not normal.

The imbalance in their relationship made mom melancholy. She obsessively sharpened dad's pencils till they became as miniscule as pips and she jotted down her mania on love billets from their wedding anniversaries. I learned the handwriting of her depression. A handwriting which was wet. And, having instinctively come to understand her suicidal need for me to be there for her, I would repeat once, from the beginning, the notes my mom would write on thin air, in order to fill the gaps of the entire family. I was the daughter who became her mom's mother.

I was afraid and, in order not to be, I came up with an idea.

I made up a set of wings.

the invention

My wings were hidden in the wardrobe for many years. My childhood wardrobe in the storeroom. They were in their depths, covered with ashes.

I was very much afraid of storms. Like a voiceless bird that quaked every time the weather turned savage and the earth was split from the sky and there was no space in between in which to fly, every time the lightning rod of the family house beat against the walls, cracked them and came inside, every time the house was split in two, I hid, every single time, inside the childhood wardrobe until everything quieted down. And everything did. Thanks to my wings.

I built a set of large improvised wings that made me not be at all afraid. I built large improvised wings and every time the storm blurred the window pane, I put on my wings and without stepping down, I danced with my lame leg held aloft, like a small ballerina, flying a red ribbon in my hands like a white flag and shaking the wings on my back to lift off, to escape from terror. And I made it. I created a breathing space. Thanks to my wings.

My parents had split the house in two, it was a habit of my dad's to covertly threaten my mom when his own power was threatened and he was afraid. He was afraid she might make him another child like me. He would wear dark woolen slippers and potter around the place, dragging darkness through the house. He would go in the library to smoke, silently closing the door behind him. The books were burning, what knowledge there had been lost in the smoke coming out of the cracks, the whole house was up in smoke, the fumes made mom dizzy and me and my dog with the one white eye and the other one black.

I remember one time he hit me in the face because I said a new word I had learned at school; "You're an arsonist and you set our house on fire on purpose" I had said to him. He had started to cry; "Why are you crying dad?" I asked, "I remembered my father", he answered, "he was a hard man, his head was grooved and ugly and he had this big wide nose in the middle cutting it in two, as if he'd come out of a horror movie, it's weird how a nose can make you so twofaced". "You shouldn't talk about your father like that, dad, that's what you say to me when you're talking dad, have some respect for your father, dad".

My father made my mother have some plastic surgery on the little knob that stuck out on top of her nose. My mother's change was unbelievable. I'm not sure what I was afraid of the most, the smoked-up room or the mutated nose. I put on my wings and put my mind at ease.

the house

There had always been two floors in the house. There was a mountain in the house.

There was water inside the house.

The house had always been split in two. The upstairs floor. The downstairs floor. In between was a huge space, as empty as a vault that would host the next body. One might say it was the family vault. Except it wasn't. The two of them manipulating their desires all those years, playacting repetitive jokes which they kept trying to figure out. The moments inside the house lasted and lasted.

One day they both found themselves on the downstairs floor. Dad in the living room. Mom in the kitchen. Nothing different happened that day. Ill equipped for preserving even a trace of memory from their disjointed common life, they were unable to understand one another.

Memory is not deceptive. You remember by forgetting. The two of them clutched onto this condition.

That day's coincidence was intimacy. Not any word spoken or the acceptance of a fleeting glance or even a touch that might reenergize, if for seconds, some of their deadened cells.

The TV on. The voice issuing from inside it, like a battle-ready monster. Always the monster in between, as father, as mother, as choice. The TV imposed its own reality and my parents theirs. No difference between the two. One more game. A game between two players.

Dad's eyes followed the course of a green ball. Silence in the court. These games impose their silence. In these games, the audience watches without sullying the site with their cries. There will be no victory, there will be no defeat. The vegetable-green ball was rolling back and forth, leaping out of the TV into the living room. Nobody seemed to be hitting it. It was following a perennial mechanical motion of its own. It bounced on the walls with force and skill and came back, bounced and came back. This repetition had turned dad's brain autistic. The living room persisted in a state of autism.

The gas stove was on. The water was boiling. Mom was inhaling. She used to sing in the past, though ever since I was born she had lost her voice. Once upon a time she was wet, vital earth, since I was born only droplets of moisture. The gas stove on, day and night.

There were two floors. The downstairs floor was the perpetrator, the upstairs floor was the victim. And the foundations of this edifice had been preserved intact through codependency.

There was a mountain inside the house. Dad was always immovable. He provoked mom, kept her in tears, and he lived through it and never met with any harm. He wouldn't be able to stand it if he lost his omnipotence.

There was water inside the house. Mom used to cry. There was fog from various water outlets.

The mountain made out the water in the far distance.

The water could smell a mountain somewhere nearby. Sensations were the last force that was still going strong.

There was force in the house. My force, which would help me save myself. Doubt had buried this force of mine in the childhood wardrobe in the basement.

Mom went up to her floor. All her forbearance went into crying spells that drizzled out. And as she climbed the stairs of the house, her brain registered that her body had dissolved in billions of water molecules and what was left was a lake disproportionately small in relation to her true size.

Dad had turned the TV off. It was late by now. His autistic thoughts banged left and right, left and right against the walls, shattering the windowpanes. His eyes appeared to be closed. He was sleepwalking while awake when he felt water around his feet. His feet got soaked. Not even at that moment did he accept responsibility for being the one primarily responsible for the breakup of the house. It was just his feet got wet.

Doubt was weaving a conspiracy and the vault was all set and moist for hosting another relationship. That of my parents.

thorns

I hadn't been scared. The first time I saw melia next to the bedside table in my room, I hadn't been scared. I felt relief and it was clear to me, for some unspecified reason that she was there because I needed her. The moment had at long last arrived for me to stop wasting myself; I didn't know it and persisted in hiding in my darkness under my woolen blanket, like a small turtle that draws its head back inside its shell, with one plausible outcome of this miserable situation being that one day I would no longer stick my head out again, as heavy sleep would have been my death.

melia for her part, was patient with me and had I refused her on that cold morning, she would have simply vanished, before I had time to reject her and I would have risen from my sleep and looked out the window at the white snow covering the slovenliness of the self-righteous city, warmth would not become familiar territory and the ice inside of me would not have melted. My heart was so frozen that I was already dead.

How could the ice melt that I inherited from my Father who abandoned me when I was far too young to understand. In my body every year of his absence grew like a thorn.

Many thorn-years on my body, were now covering a large part of its surface. While growing up, I learned not to lean against others so I wouldn't scratch them. I isolated in my room and observed the quality of suffering. I was young then and, for a writer, suffering is a good departure point provided you haven't managed to turn it into a virtue.

There was no therapy that could remove my thorns. I positioned myself with difficulty wherever it was I needed to lean on. I didn't change positions so as not to cause pain. My relationship with thorns was a love-hate one. Could it be possible for me not to hurt so much?

The night before melia's visit, I dared think that I do not love pain. I opened the drawer of the bedside table and stood looking at my writings for hours. How to break the silence? Every year a thorn, every thorn a text, every text a silence and the silence anger. I was very angry.

melia took a small scalpel on that freezing morning and with a gardener's care, snipped the points off my thorns. I surrendered like a baby incapable of responding. It took her a while. She meticulously removed all the most pointed edges to the part where the root started to show. Then, she took a file and started filing around the circumference of each root.

As soon as she had finished filing, she made me look at myself in the mirror. The roots of Father's thorns, infantile volcanoes ready to explode. I touched them in order to get a new sense of my body when, up till then, I had conceived of deformity as the only truth. I was someone else. Yet, my peculiarity still remained visible, only covered by new attributes. There was me and my shadow on the back wall twice as large, while melia was nowhere in the mirror.

Before she even spoke to me, I asked, raging with anger, if there were others like me and then I started to cry, unable to stop.

She hugged me. I felt intense prickling. It wasn't her heart, or mine. It was her thorns, the thorns of her own family story which, had I not heard from her own mouth, I would not have been able to write.

I held her away from me.

What part of myself spoke my truth so courageously? In the shadow up on the wall, I saw the young child. He had his eyes closed, his underwear was lowered and he was having piss with a contraction that was neither pleasurable nor painful. The ice had started to melt. I had been able to cry.

writer-subject relationship

There were no mistakes in their attained spelling of wholeness. There was no worm in the watermelon. There was no vertigo unto life or fervor unto death between them. They did not become lovers, they were never going to be.

the ice

I was a nine year old boy when my Father died. melia's care brought that memory back with a vengeance. That summer day the ground had become frozen. I dug worms out of the dirt, small, large, huge ones, and put them in a row until they became canals in which the running water of the garden tap flowed like a river. Then, I took the kittens of mother's cat and let them wander inside the long branching construction until they found the way out on their own.

After a while, I took the tortured, drowned baby kittens and hid them again under the bed, on my Father's side, inside my patent leather shoes, covered up with the pair of shorts I wore on the day of his funeral.

"He is small and handsome, a good boy and a quiet one", were the descriptions I had grown up with for the past nine years of my life; "he plays all by himself in the garden and doesn't bother anyone", my mother used to say about her son.

Every night, I would curl up on Father's side of the bed, sniffing at the death I had been growing underneath the bed after he was gone. Until the day when the dirt was frozen by an unexpected, evil frost in the heart of summer, which caught my childish motives unawares and put a stop to my obsessive drowning of the kittens of mother's cat, who had been giving birth non-stop, a silent accomplice my revenge.

The ground was frozen solid.

Through the frosted windowpane my improvised construction with the many canals looked pointless. Having smothered all traces of my anger, I found myself in a state of immobilization – that lasted for years – admiring my creation with the incomprehension of a puzzled child. The incomprehension caused me to cry a great deal. My crying melted the ice. I leant against my shelf and went to sleep. That was the last time I'd cried.

My mother was looking for me for a long time before she found me in the ice.

She picked me up in her arms and took me to her bed, on Father's, which I had unwittingly taken possession of. She kept me warm until my temperature returned to normal.

My mother kept warming me for a long time and her breath used to cause me an unacknowledged tremor of panic. Because her breath, her torrential kisses later on and my horrid hand inside of her, tasted like the warm discharge of a deadly orgasm.

As soon as my eyes were open, I lowered my head to look under the bed, terrorized. There were no drowned kittens. There was no trace of death.

My mother never spoke of it. Until such time as I turned adult and was assured that this was only a nightmare bequeathed by my Father on the day he left me an orphan. My mother never did speak to me about the two of us and our relationship which had defiled my Father's bed.

I never again cried in front of my mother. A great many years passed, looped together with myself as the missing link. melia had allowed me to be angry and for that reason, I loved her at that moment more than anyone else.

the laundry

I was calm. A storm had left the room all moist. I was dry.
I felt better. So many years had gone by that I had lost all
sense of how long they'd lasted.

melia had shifted position in space. The freezing days
of winter had warmed the weather with their passing and,
if you touched the windowpane, you would feel your palms
cared for by its mellow temperature.

She held in her hand a white button she'd just taken out
of her purse. She was having difficulty breathing as if parts
of life were waking up inside her which she had decided
to keep from me.

She opened the window, a warm cold came into the small
room, she threw out the white button, closed the window.

A ray of sunlight pierced the windowpane of the two-
story house across the street where my small room was. The
light's reflection came back and illuminated melia's form.
She had her back turned and I was only able to see her face
reflected in the glass of the two-story house across the street
where a woman lived whom I didn't know.

The unknown woman with the red hair and the
accentuated bust was on the balcony hanging out her

laundry. I couldn't see clearly, the street separating the two houses was narrow, the distance seemed great to me, my unfocused eyes trained on the stretched line with the sparkling clothes on it, the smell of their cleanliness wafted into my small room reminding me that I had been innocent once. I got distracted for a little while.

Full of innocence – a privilege I hadn't had access to for years – I saw the clothes shaken up one by one disgorging mice, geese, squirrels, a pregnant cow and a thick swarm of bees which spread like dust for kilometers around, making a sound with the nutritional value of royal jelly. Myriads of queen bees commuted around in my universe and, for some peculiar reason, this commotion of theirs was well familiar to me.

As soon as melia turned and looked at me, the picture of the unknown woman started fading and the laundry stayed in place, secured by the clothespins, releasing droplets of water like melting stalactites. I felt happiness. How pretty, how pretty.

For a moment, it crossed my mind that melia doesn't exist, that I had dreamt her up and that was when her voice picked up the telling of her story.

the button

Her parents' relationship made it difficult for her to communicate with them. A shortness of breath of psychological origin which she'd kept secret and which caused her to lose contact with the environment, was the first consequence of the family anxiety she'd had to face.

She was afraid of the button. An ordinary white button, the very top one that does up the front of the neck, coming right after the zipper that did up the school uniform.

She was done with school many years now. That had been a time when girl students still wore uniforms. Blue ones. So had she. She still has the nightmare of the school uniform button every night. The one that constricted her neck and made her unable to breathe normally. Resulting in a shortness of breath of psychological origin.

At six she would put on the blue uniform every morning, glancing at the button in horror. She knew that when she did it up, it would deprive her of freedom, would imprison the maturity she had single handedly cultivated despite her youth, in recompense for the lack of family succor. When faced with her parents, she was terror stricken. They disputed every thought before she had uttered it and this was the reason why she kept her words to herself, never letting them out of her mouth.

She stroked the button so it would relax, she pulled at the collar to increase its girth, she stared at it every morning, on the off-chance it might take pity on her.

The button, like mom, like dad, like the teachers, was always at its appointed place. The girl was asking it to shift its position a bit, give her some breathing space. No drastic change ever took place.

School came to an end, the uniform was no longer required, melia pulled at the button to break it off. She carried it in her purse. She'd promised to throw it out along with the psychological shortness of breath.

Why now, I asked her. She was silent.

While her silence lasted, she was looking persistently into my eyes trying to decide whether I was worthy of knowing the whole truth, whether I was able to not doubt her. When she made her choice, she spoke.

If you read the diary my mom kept, there won't be much of a reason left for me to talk about her. She was the only person who intuited the difficulty of my survival, given I don't possess a brain. But mom was a wolf with the behavior of a tethered dog, weak and laconic. The tied-up dog does not have a will and after a

time, doesn't even know if it has any desires of its own, except at night it dreams of the wolf, powerful and free. Mom could not abide the wolf and so she refused him. She refused the monstrosity she'd given birth to and after that, she fell silent. I limped. My faith reassured me that nobody was going to tie me to a pole.

Every morning as I waited for mom to wake up, I stared at the round belly, her protruding navel and I repeated

I love you, I love you, I love you, I love you, mom

and as soon as she let out a roar like a baby lion rolling in the wheat under the sun, I abruptly stopped and I came to.

Because I was lying.

I didn't love my mom.

relationship of writer to subject

I don't think I've ever felt love. I have never loved any speaking being. I didn't love me, I didn't love dad, I didn't love my husband, I wasn't able to love my children. What melia loves in everyone is not themselves but the wolf inside of them.

the diary

I got back home late. I had been hiding in the roots of the red tree again. No one can find me there.
He was asleep. I fell asleep as well. I think he woke me up in the night and was saying something, can't remember what. The pills have decimated my perception. He interrupted my sleep.

I got up and went to the room of the little girl. She is feverish. I picked her and carried her to the conjugal bed. I sent him off to sleep in the little girl's bed. He slept in the living room. I sent him to sleep in the little girl's bed because the truth is I can only go to sleep next to her. The pills have decimated my perception. In the morning I gutted an orange.

In my sleep I heard the little one. She was talking out loud. I was exhausted. I didn't get up. In my state of deprivation my limbs were delirious, listening was all I was capable of.

The little one was negotiating with the house keeper what she was going to have for lunch.
Can she think?

I gutted an orange.

The little girl wakes up early before me, she usually sits quietly on the bedside table and watches me until I too am awake. I mean she does not leave the room, I mean she does not wake me up, I mean she stays by my side until I open my eyes. Which I sometimes do not do, hiding instead underneath my woolen blanket for fear of seeing her there before me.
Dark-colored, lusterless, small, bitter.

He said to me "don't take these, these are addictive".
I said to him "but they can't possibly be worse for me than you are".

He said to me "it's not a question of the effect they have, it's your dependency on them".

In the morning I got up, asked for pills. I stopped short just in the nick of time, thought of dependency and drew back.

In the afternoon I asked for pills. I stopped short just in the nick of time,

thought of dependency for a second time and drew back.

In the evening I asked for pills. I stopped panic stricken and drew back.

He called for an ambulance to come get me, I went in to detox.

I was incarcerated, I had no desire to urinate, to defecate or to sleep for long hours. I think I must have had a mistaken perception of the movements of my limbs. I attempted to masturbate twice when I thought of him and I was unsuccessful.

They served me my favorite food, they said good morning to me every morning at nine and they said goodnight every evening at nine. I didn't mind that the room was empty and white or that its size was two square meters by two. In there I discovered that I can think.

I thought of the will I'm going to leave, Melia at school and how pretty she looks in her blue uniform, the ignominies I have committed against myself, the loans

I have outstanding, whether the housekeeper presses my shirts correctly. I thought of the bad relationship I had with my father's second wife. I thought of my mother, of the oranges I've gone without.

That dream in which I died every time, made me cry every harsh night:

"I'm a wolf prowling in my cage. My claws, my teeth and my fur keep getting longer and longer, my skin is one huge blister, the retinas in my eyes are multiplying. I have horns that are crooked, ingrown ones, so mutated that they pierce my head down to the root making it bleed. Wet nostrils opening and closing every few seconds. Every time in the dream, they put me to sleep by injection. They feed me orange juice subcutaneously. I hear them say

"it is very sick, it hurts when you touch it"

"recently, it's as if it's lost its mind, it doesn't eat, doesn't drink, doesn't talk" "it seems old, it's young in years"

"how long has it been in this cage?" "it was born here"

"what do you want me to do?"

"spare it the suffering, if we let it loose it will devour all of us"

"Do you believe that?"

"Kill it painlessly before it understands the meaning of the silence".

When my episodes grew less frequent and then stopped, they told me I was free.

I went outside knowing that he wouldn't be waiting, to my great surprise he was hanging around the street corner with a small puppy as a gift for me.

The morning is bare without coffee, because my mind needs its fuel. I am absolutely addicted to the drug morning-coffee. A dark colored sip for every tortuous hour needed for every day to be over and done with.

He was ready to leave for work. He again put on his lettuce green shoes. I managed to get up at dawn when he'd be at home. I had a conversation with him, told him that his behavior alienates me. He didn't speak. As soon as he was gone, I went to the sink to look at his coffee cup with the dark leftovers at the bottom. I hate seeing that. The housekeeper will wash up.

The housekeeping woman has a cough. I told her she shouldn't go out in the cold to wash down the yard every day... the dog keeps pissing at the house entrance and the black stains of his shit, their stench comes in through the nostrils exciting the brain.... she answered that she cleans up after the dog.

I must sort through the clothes of the little one. There's need for some space in the child's wardrobe. Give away the clothes she's outgrown so other children can make use of them.

We ate, each family member at a different time, I then put on the long coat over the pajamas and went for a walk in the yard. I hid in the roots of the red tree again. No one can find me there. The little one was happy, she was playing with the dog.

I'm thinking that the housekeeping woman isn't happy here that I am not good enough to her. I won't talk to her. I can't bear for her to leave. She takes good care of the little one. I am on a permanent diet.

Am on a permanent diet.

On a permanent diet.

A permanent diet.

Permanent diet.

Diet.

I fell asleep again.
Around 8pm the little one woke me up. We sat, the two girls together, to see a fairytale on TV. She said, "mom, I can't see it by myself, come with me, because when I touch you you're like a house, come mommy".

The fever is up again.

He put on his lettuce green shoes, I told him the blue ones suit him. He put on the lettuce green ones. He reminded me to take the dog for its rabies injection. I laughed. I looked at him puzzled. I said to him: "if I was an elephant and you hugged me, you'd realize your size, if I was a pink elephant you wouldn't care about my size but about my color". He doesn't understand. He looked at me puzzled.

I told him: "I'm no pink elephant". He still didn't understand anything. I lit my cigarette and sat on the edge of the couch. The farthest edge. Again he didn't hug me. He drummed his fingers on the table.

The TV was playing the same fairytale tonight as well.

Repetitiveness.

Autism.

The light behind us delineated our outlines on the glass. Wasn't I in this
fairytale?

My mouth smelled of cigarettes and stale sperm. Every time I take him in my mouth, I get the taste of other vaginas. The room smelled of worn couch.

I saw the blue shoes on their own in a corner and I used them to dress my naked feet.

I slept with the little one. Up close to her, it's warm. She holds my hand and her certainty gives me strength. I ate an orange.

The housekeeper has the day off today. The house hasn't been taken care of. The girl has on tiny finger-puppets and she's playing with them.
He is always away.

My head hurts very much. I'm getting goose bumps in my scull. The pills aren't helping.

I sit alone in the kitchen rocking chair with the balcony door open so that air can get in and I am gutting an orange. First the juice, then the seams, then the peel. The orange is decimated inside of me.
From the kitchen I can see the library, the yard. The dog is in the yard, looking at me, I'd like for it to live inside the house but he won't let me. Seeing he's away, I'll let the dog in.
Nobody needs me now.

the unconscious

For a long time melia would refuse to talk about her mom and also about being a mother herself. There was no conscious utterance possible about the truth contained in the impasse of motherhood. She felt alienated from her children just as she had from her mother. The perverse dependency of melia's mom had caused their roles to reverse.

When she was young, people said she looked like her mom. She had mom's attitude, copied her mannerisms. Did she feel ok with that?

Her childhood had run into her veins like toxic blood, flowing from the head down into the stomach for many years, in an attempt to be processed.

She was aware that the lucky ones are those who can glimpse their life for one single moment and then, when faced with the choice to sink or swim, that one moment becomes a raft.

Her intuition had become stronger. Though still young in years, she knew that the thing of value was not the moment of birth or death but her passage from the one to the other. She hadn't feared her birth, hadn't feared her incomprehensible form, she would not fear her death. But she was at odds with the fear of life she was experiencing.

She was determined to have a few moments of happiness.

the need

Such as the first time melia had plunged her hand inside the white cotton underpants. She had no recollection of it. Nor of the second time or the one after that. An ordinary need through the years, like peeing. She wanted it where she expected it. A need providing momentary relief.

She had peed herself as a baby and only the housekeeper, who tended to objects and people alike, knew about it. The woman scolded her for losing control and she grew fearful of this particular human need. Until, that is, it was cut short once and for all, like a knife cutting an orange in half.

By the time she had grown out of her child's cotton briefs, her unspeakable thoughts were causing her to soil her underwear without her hand's intervention.

She took on board the satisfaction which a transgressive thought can provide. When one such arrived, she would grab a lock of her hair and twist it painfully until the underwear was all stained. She 'd let out a sound like the whoosh of a single exhalation and that moment of beneficence towards her own self, would fill her with an fleeting recognition of her own existence.

Satisfaction, at last. This was a fair relationship. One about which nobody had the right to scold her. A relationship without desire, oaths, supervision, risk, drama, guilt. She registered that, in order to love herself, the reverse had to happen first. Every act of masturbation secured the boundaries of a place where she alone was authorized to enter.

The red tree in whose roots melia's mom hid, did not change place. Trees don't.

Mom grew darker with the years, hiding under the woolen blanket. The fallen red leaves by her feet seemed as dark as bull's blood.

melia's dad visibly indifferent to his wife's depression and to that abomination, his daughter, was away. He left the house at dawn with the idea of a desirable child and returned in the dark of night, hoping a miracle might have taken place. He would slowly enter meila's room, slowly bend over her, survey her outer shell which in appearance, was complete, pretty, alive, and, once he was certain melia was fast asleep, would guiltily, disbelievingly, kiss her forehead. This was all he gave of himself.

Guilty and disbelieving because it was "difficult" for him to point out the culprit. Whose fault was the girl's abnormality? How is it possible that you can think, melia? And what is the source which feeds your mind?

A father is a good father until his child is presented to him. This one dad, however, wasn't given the time to make an effort. His own weakness wounded him. Every night he stood observing his daughter, trying to fathom his genes. That was his aim, nothing else. melia's mind belonged to her like the earth belongs to itself. Except for many years her mind would be in error, taking onto itself the responsibility for everything. The damage done claimed so much space inside of her that it would take a long time again to admit to all the mistakes she'd made, trying to please everyone except her own self. She hung on to two dangerous conditions, for mom not to leave, for dad to come back.

That kiss of dad's, just that.

melia slowly lifted her arm and took hold of a lock of her hair. She started twisting it until her scalp started to hurt.

By the time she was done, the outline of her body had expanded. Her rainfall had come inside the small room.

She looked me brightly in the eye and smiled and winked. Then, she hopped onto the bed and started talking.

the dream

Those nights when I lay bundled in bed with dad sitting a hair's breadth away, my senses were roused. As I pretended to be asleep, my youthful heart wailed in anguished fear that he might not kiss me. I needed that kiss and without it, his indifference stifled me. I didn't want to lose him. If I lost dad, I would lose my power, that's what I believed. He so wanted for me to be male. I had to take on a masculine form in order not to disappoint him. At nights, in my small room, there was only enough space for me and for him. And though I wanted him to stay on, he did, always, leave.

Every night in my dream, the echo of another self, familiar but also terrible, took on the form of a dark angel who started talking to me with a voice not my own and, as he did, I was ejected into a place where I uttered my first syllables. The dark angel shone from head to foot and chords of light extended out from his arteries, lighting up my words until I would faint.

In my dream, I had a head, a torso, a belly, two antennae between two compound eyes to the sides and three simple eyes on the top part of my head. Two pairs of membranous wings grew from my body. I was the perfect insect, the perfect queen bee. I was closer to my distortion than any other time and I was happy. Was this me?

The dark angel stood over me, looking like mom's depression, and observed the queen. He didn't have the right to take her life away.

With his next loving kiss I would come to, I would pierce his soul with my sting and watch him transform from dark angel to saint.

But, wait, queen bees have no sting, I had the audacity to interject. Sorry, my mistake.

The voice trailed off softly, leisurely repeating the same words always, leaving behind a creaking sound which woke me up to subject me again to the silence.

By the time I was adolescent, my dad would come into my room kiss me, walk out again. I'd get up in the dark, peer at my toes that were so much like his own and, leaning on my crooked leg, I'd search for his woolen slippers. I would light a cigarette in secret without smoking it. I thought a smoky room, which was a habit of his, would bring him back to me. He would see a part of him in me and he would know. I was flirting with his ghost, not the real him. I was flirting with the man who accepted me as I was because, due to his absence, he'd never had to face me, and so to hurt me. The cigarette as a substitute of my unnamed thoughts, perched in the slit of my half-opened lips. This was how I was taking my revenge on him.

Every morning, my hand would spontaneously rise to pile my hair on top of my head with a clip, leaving the nape of the neck bare so as to relish the aftereffect of the kiss.

The first sense I ever had of an identity of my own was the love I wanted to believe my dad felt for me. A secret black wedding ring which I savagely shoved to the back of the brain I didn't have.

Each morning my desire took me into my parents' bedroom to see him. To see what he was like in the morning, when the mind is clearer. Dad was never there. Then, there was nothing else for me to think, and I would sit by my mother, numb and empty, until it was time for her to wake up, while the hours of waiting for dad's return magnified, sculpting out a sad truth inside of me.

Love turned into darkness. Dad taught me the form my lovers would take upon my body. In every act of lovemaking, by body's shape tightened, my body's skin roughened, the internal organs atrophied like children lacking for food and water. I was fearful of such negotiations, my capacity to trust was impaired. The word "love" took the place of the word "difficult" and every man I desired assumed dad's characteristics. The erotic act took on a bipolar meaning for me. I made so many mistakes that I couldn't even like myself.

I tried hard. I tried to locate my disordered self in between the relationships I had and the truth I was looking for myself. I wasn't going to be able to negotiate on the basis of lies anymore and so I thought of him as dead, though he wasn't. I went silent. Not like mom's day-to-day silence or the silence of his absence, but a different silence, an incarceration of wanting, the silence of words trapped in writings. I lived inside writing.

I divided in two. My sadness and the expectation of my non-sadness. What privileges were there for me to avail myself of?

At nineteen, all of that changed.

the separation

It was their nineteenth wedding anniversary. Mom had set up dinner for two. No tablecloth, mom had just discovered place mats. With animal patterns and horrible, embossed sculls from some exotic trip they'd gone on. Black porcelain plates with fine white dots, carefully positioned in the center. Cutlery ending in serpent tails tied in a knot. Wine glasses in different sizes, the taller one for dad, the shorter for mom, the thinner one for dad's water, the thick one for mom's.

On each plate was featured a plastic animal from my childhood collection. She had a habit of placing my animals on the guest's dinner plates for them to find their place by guessing which animal they were.

At that dinner, she'd placed a plastic jackass in dad's place and in her own, a plastic sow. Red candles burned all night. Red geraniums, her favorite, accentuated the atmosphere of a family brothel.

I have an image of mom from just before I went up to my room. An unusual image of a pretty, well-groomed woman. My father, too, had shaved and put on his wedding tie.

Dinner started as soon as I fell asleep.

I've no idea what happened before I was woken up by a disturbing nightmare. The plastic animals of my childhood had come alive. The jackass brayed till it was out of breath, the sow devoured everything it could and then some, and I was a little lost dragon frantically looking for my kingdom.

I 've no idea what happened before I woke up and found myself curled up on the landing secretly watching my parents' celebration of their anniversary.

Funnily, I remember nothing from that evening. I have no image of dad or mom, only of the cake with the candles still burning and melting and my bulimia the next day, wanting to eat it all so there'd be no trace of it left. Dad and mom separated a few months later.

I was the one who experienced the "difficultness" of my parents' separation, since there was no ground for mutual understanding or acceptance, even after they'd split up. As far as I was concerned, there was always a meeting point between two people. If two people are defined as two points, there is always intermediary space. It may be void, it may be common, or it may be another point. The intermediary space between my parents would forever be me.

I accepted their separation. I did not accept my father's leaving. Being deprived of his kiss was painful. He had abandoned me. With mom. He had abandoned me to fear.

Inside of me a crevice was opening up. What if he had, once, drawn a boat for me on the windowpane of my room, a boat that lit up the dark sky at night, where the moon and stars made promises of an extraordinary future? I was now shipwrecked in that future.

I knew their bedroom door had been broken a long time now, someone had lost the key, broken the handle, let the hinges go rusty, let the door come undone and so it did, it shifted and ended up leaning against the beam, heavy and unmoving; the light from their bedroom chandelier cast around new reflections, illuminating new corners, leaving old ones in the dark, creating a corridor of novel information.

On the night of their separation, my parents had unexpectedly ejected their most heartfelt fears outside the family bowl like elderly fish throwing themselves out of the sea, gasping for breath.

relationship of writer to subject

The story is one only, it is re-inscribed many times in order to acquire a specific form, a specific structure. In the beginning, you are taught letters in order to write, you write in order to get a voice, then you are taught letters in order to read, readings of your own which take care of the fragments and, in the end, there is only the others' reading vis-a-vis your own writing, since reading never does coincide with writing. There are secretive readers, too, ones that take on the observer's role. One such is me, Chris.

the writings

As my frame of mind changed, melia gradually transformed into an unexpectedly beautiful woman. Had I not heard her story, I wouldn't have accepted that we had a single ugly trait in common.

Till the death of my Father everything was childlike. Behind the light was the house where I grew up.

It had sky inside it or, rather, I saw sky inside it because I could not see sky in the sky.

In the sky I could only see clouds, stars, airplanes and birds, the sun and the moon, but never any sky.

It confused me, the sky that was nowhere to be seen, but only existed as *sky* to speak of and hear about it whenever others made a reference.

I wanted to, and I so did, put sky inside the house over the colors of the walls.

I wanted to, and so I did, also put sky on marble floors, inside wardrobes, on shelves, in the TV, in the pots, in the weave of the clothes, in the folds of the curtain, in the faucets, in the heating and the air-conditioning, under the roof tiles and inside the chimney and higher up than the chimney.

I wanted to, and so I did, put sky inside the people of the house,

inside grandfather who counted the lentils one by one before we ate them, inside grandmother who'd turned blind by everything she had seen,

inside my little sister who suddenly grew adult teeth in the place of her baby ones, inside my mother who laughed immodestly and looked at me hesitantly,

inside my Father whom I'd spent next to no time with.

He was always away on trips and when he came back, he traced ships on the windows, triangular, square and oblong ships travelling on erased seas and after the end of every story, he would improvise on what happened next.

More than anywhere, I had put light inside the ships. The ships and the erased seas.

At night, I looked out the window, watching a sea that didn't exist, the shapes of ships that sailed to nowhere. And always by my side, my dog with one white eye and one black.

And I wrote. So the light came alive. And I had a question. Father, is there fault in writing?

I wrote letters to my imaginary friend who would be an unexpectedly beautiful

woman, and I was waiting for her. My friend was always away but I didn't mind because in my mind I had created my imaginary family filled with light.

I used to cover my writings with a child's warm, white, cotton little blanket and leave them laid out on the table like fragile human bones till my friend was due to turn up. My dog sniffed politely at the bones, he recognized them as mine and didn't mess with them, the sea outside the window remained erased.

I would go to sleep. I would have a dream.

I see the little white blanket wrapping itself around me like a shroud and dragging me to the bottom of the sea which is the only place where I can breathe.

I see myself, a human-a mummy-a fish

I see scattered letters swimming around me without forming any words the part of the sea bottom where I lie is ticking like a clock counting the minutes during which I can live differently

I see my friend arrive on a ship

I see her casting nets trying to fish me out

I see her taking me out on shore

I wake up

I look at the table

I see scattered bones from my Father's exhumation.

I'd wake up tired.

the burial

Boys don't cry. Still, I used to wet myself out of fear till the age of nine. I didn't feel sadness or pleasure. I only felt a numbness because there hadn't been time for me to save my relationship with my father.

I would look out the window and see snow falling. It had buried the ship-shapes, it had buried the sea. The snow reflected its light off me and I knew that everything I needed in order to escape was buried deep inside me. I sat impassively waiting for someone who was never coming back.

My Father had deserted me to my mother's immodest laughter. My dog, a guardian that kept me mentally lucid. My days were black and white like its eyes. There were days when my life was full of light and days when my life was full of darkness. And in the darkness, mother's voice ruled.

You mustn't cry. You are never to cry again. Like a preternatural leech, perversion had nestled on her skin. The leech was sucking on mother's blood and she was sucking on mine.

I would fall sleep in her arms and, as I slept, I could feel the leech cover the surface of my child's body, infiltrating every pore. It drained me.

Exhausted, I would keep my eyes shut so tightly that I saw the flames of Eastern candles burning and mother's cat dressed in red sharpening its teeth with its claws and through its eyes throw javelins on our two incestuous bodies, taking revenge on the tormentor of her slaughtered kittens. She had no forgiveness to spare on a murderer such as myself, and no interest whatsoever in the motives behind my action.

Mother kept the leech a secret. For every morning she would look at me with the empty, hollow eyes of an old woman, as if the night had not existed, and then she'd laugh immodestly and explosively to my face.

One time while she laughed, the disgust I felt for our relationship caused me a crying fit. I was crying obsessively like a child who wants his mother back, only she's lost the way and can't make it back to him. I cried like a child and she, without the training to handle my child's crying, hit me. It hurt and I was stopped short, staring down at her adult's shoes that were teaching me how to make my way in life.

I shouldn't cry. Not even when I hurt. I learned the secret as a young boy - I had to satisfy my mother and I needed to find a way to do it.

I was a child and I had become an adolescent, I had become a man, I had become a lover, I'd become a husband, I had become a Father.

Those were ill-omened times. Despicable. The falls and winters, each spring all wrong, the summers as well.

relationship of writer to subject

Everything is well covered up!

the loss

A thick white sheet covered the floor space. The whiteness of the ice was pure, calm with the darkness of the cold hidden inside it.

An unbalanced feeling was seeping into my cortex. I sensed without knowing it that I wasn't truly unhappy. Father's death stopped time at number nine. How many years had passed since then? I wasn't good with numbers. I wasn't quite grown to where I could solve the riddles of arithmetic.

Dear God, how lacking in training I was! I had resigned myself to the imaginary and fed myself on a language of my own, self-created, that inflicted cunning bites without leaving any marks of proof.

I seemed fragile and strange, not quite normal. Out of my mouth came the sounds of words that hovered somewhere between the real world and the imaginary one I was experiencing. I missed Father and my sounds were calling to him, though not even mother understood the incomprehensibility of my loss.

I had even forgotten how to say my actual name. There's much I do remember and more than anything how I kept running after him on my little legs. It saddens me not to remember the sound of his voice, despite his words "not even the gods can escape fate; don't come after me, don't follow on my footsteps".

I didn't mean to, but I felt alone at home, and scared. The nights after his death, the old empty table creaked, the old wardrobe creaked, the conjugal bed with me and my mother on it creaked. And the door to the courtyard swiveled with a heavy, grating sound. The nights when the hot darkness squashed the last filaments of free-floating air, the pot with the unnaturally red, gigantic geraniums cast a strange, elongated shadow on the wall.

When once, as I was looking at the shadow I asked "mom, where is Father?" she gave me two resounding slaps, imprinting her rough maternal palm on my cheeks. I didn't ask again. That night my mother woke out of a feverish spell and cried "I hate him, how I hate him". It was then that I heard for the first time how much mother hated Father. I had been wrong to believe that I was the cause of her revenge.

And I was always present, always there so she could manage through the extension of the man who'd fathered me, that part of masculinity he had deprived her of. I can accept she had some responsibility. But how aware can a mother be as to the responsibility she bears? I do not forgive her, nor pity her.

I was still too young to know the connection between truth and action. My mother was the best audience every time I acted the part she wanted from me, that of her lover. What I wanted was to be her son, which is a truth that upset her.

The most terrible act I ever did was to split myself in two, the self I would keep for me and the male traineeship I undertook, which I generously and heartrendingly offered to my mother.

On those occasions when I would wake up with a clear mind, a need greater than thought started prompted me to write. I became the writer of my incarceration and of my freedom. I recorded freedom as an antidote for all the times when I had to negotiate the "difficultness" of Father's death; and I recorded incarceration as a safekeep, as evidence proving the perversity which my mother had visited on me.

I was so young.

I was so young that I had named the fish in Father's aquarium with sounds, the small fish was dzvoo, the large was bloo, the one larger still was shroo, and there was yet another one of indeterminate size, female and gilded with slit eyes and gauzy fins, which I'd named melia. One day it just suddenly disappeared out of the aquarium.

the fairytale

melia was listening to me attentively. She possessed this incredible gift of being there when I needed her, after a long time of sadness which I'd hidden under my heavy woolen blanket. I hadn't invited her but it didn't even cross my mind to wonder about her sudden presence in the room. Her name belonged to the language of my childhood and so melia's familiarity was something I was sure of.

I had been silenced for many years. Now, with no apparent cause, I was mouthing sounds that escaped my surface like bubbles, dissolving all my guilt.

melia was listening attentively to the story of the child that grew up under the greatest adversity.

"There was a young child trying to reach a spring to drink golden water. Its frozen fingers were about to fall off. But he didn't need them because he had wrists.

The young child climbed the tallest mountain, looked down to see mother. There was no mother, "for nothing" the child thought, so much effort for nothing. High up in the stars, though, a girl sat on a cloud peeling oranges, birds were hatching eggs in midair, orange peels and eggshells covered the face of the atmosphere.

White rain was sprouting from the ground, "some things happen in reverse"

==melia told me intervening== "some things happen in reverse" I repeated back to melia. The young child doesn't yet know what terrible thing is going to happen to him. His age has value and he preserves it in the manner of an angel combing his wings.

And there, between heaven and earth, the mission was accomplished. Umbilical cords appeared out of the rooftops of buildings and started to grow alarmingly and to intertwine like a spider's web, aiming to reach for the child and strangle it, while battle-ready phalluses flew on broomsticks at devilish speed in order to save the child. Magical sacs opened and started hurling bombs in the shape of fists. In the morning it happened so and in the evening it happened in reverse. They showed him their weapons, prompting him to battle.

He was a young boy, just a young boy.

And in all the furor of war and while everyone was killing in defense of life, he – a young child – shut his eyes hard and hung on to duration, a medicine to heal his wounds.

Quietly, his mind dreamt of his heart. An invented real heroine and her voice emerged from within him. The sound of her name like a red geranium. His breath took on the smell of warm, freshly baked, chocolate cookies.

The war came to a standstill. The moment passed. But somewhere, there is a golden spring and a tall mountain and a young boy growing to adulthood through the greatest adversity".

I said and fell silent.

She started to laugh loudly and merrily as if she'd just heard the funniest story. I understand, is all she said through peals of laughter that worked like a potion that soothed my vulnerable body.

the fear

The only thing I knew about myself was my name, melia.

Then I abandoned my family home.

My parents were like two misshapen figures in space, taking up all of it. I was only destined to fit in the narrow cracks of space left by the two shapes. I crawled under, over and in between as the shapes shifted in different directions. The female shape with short hair and inverted nipples that didn't breastfeed me was mom, the male shape with short hair and lacking the gift of communication was dad.

Later – away from the family context – I understood how two shapes so castrated and dysfunctional could have assumed such bulk, weight and power in my young mind. I understood that, for years, I had myself been cultivating a self that belonged exclusively in the care of these two shapes. And this quality of mine was very much acquired, a self-willed need for survival, a need to open a space where there was none for me.

As long as I looked after my parents' space, it slowly grew larger, eating up even more of my own margin. My inept breathing which up until then, was due to an atmosphere void of oxygen, started becoming more dysfunctional. Each in-breath pushed me closer to the door, until I opened it and there was the way out.

I got out. Once out the door, I felt good. The outside seemed to me like unexplored space. How had I been focused on the two shapes only, and for so many years, and how necessary had I been to them, for them to accept it?

You too can escape when you want to. And that can be just the beginning.

My appetite felt like greed to me and my legs felt like they could be useful not just for crawling but for running far, covering great distances. I started to run. Away. As far away as I could. I didn't have the slightest idea what I was running away from. I didn't have the slightest idea about whether I would ever stop running and what my destination might be at any given point. For the shape that was following me, having assumed gigantic proportions was my own, that indeterminate one, pushing me into a mental debauchery where my only recourse against its action was to punish my body so that it hurt more than my soul.

The only thing I knew about myself till then was my name, meiia. Who are my parents?

My mom and my dad. What have I been?

Me.

Who gave birth to me? My mom.

Who brought me up? My dad's absence.

Who taught me? Grandma's teachings.

love relations

My grandmother was the first to speak to me about the idea of a lover. It was in all of her stories. My grandmother had dementia.

Lovers were traces, a part of my mind that fed my body. Without them my body atrophied, constricted, swelled up, went into imbalance, withered. Without that experience, my body was ignorant and ignored.

I had the very first experience when I had gone into grandma's elevator. That claustrophobic one that, like a small coffin, would take me from one floor to another long before I had found its button and was able to pilot its course.

An elevator's course measures the distance separating the relics of Saint Paul and those of Cerberus. The keys to the relic-case are those of the elevator. My grandmother was Acheron, the river through which the dead cross to the other side.

Grandma's elevator, dressed in reddish wood almost always kept a warm temperature between feet and toes and bellies and armpits and breasts and backs and necks and fingerprints on its entry-exit.

The elevator of the ill-defined smell, exuded orange and patchouli and meatball and eggplant and garlic and meat and fish and fart and brilliantine and rotting tooth and worn woolen suit and silk and snakeskin purse and lollipop and freshly shampooed hairs.

Into the elevator had gone an old maestro, a young woman of mixed blood, the Holy Mother's girdle belt made of camelhair, St. John the Baptist, a butterfly broach with a broken clip, a man with a gold Christian cross on his collar bone, a man with George Batailles in his hands and myself along with them.

I was an adolescent at that time, of an age where I couldn't sleep because of too much nervous excitement, still a novice at erotic self-suggestion and feeling awkward about the thoughts I was having and could not control. I remember erotic feelings burrowing like worms inside my mind and growing into butterflies that lack all awareness of how short- lived their existence will be. That time at the beginning I thought I was falling in love.

I watched myself, touched myself and half smiled.

Woman, her image, her selves, her lovers and dad. Always dad. I observed everything I saw and identified it with the body I was touching. But was I that same person? Was I all the pairs of eyes observing me? Was it possible for me to handle so many double risks, so many imposed regimes of viewing? Was it possible for so many Others to inhabit the one body, the one entity, mine?

I had been away from home for a while and had installed myself in an attic dressed in reddish wood paneling. The attic overflowed with lovers, bodies making sounds and after every act, their ghosts would stay behind, stalking. In the dark of my few hours' sleep, the dark angel of depression would come to the head of the bed and take up dad's post of observation.

The love relations I struck up were thick disorderly vapors taking up all my bodily spaces, setting deeply into all the organs starting with the intestines, moving to the gall bladder, the stomach, the heart.

Their first penetration was like a collision. The second like a forced swallow. The third was the impression of an imprint where all the body's motions are contained.

Where was my body in lovemaking?

Where was its grave? So I could unbury it, so it could concede to pleasure, with no guilt, no guilt.

My inner body became a trespassed asylum, my outer body was tottering on the edge of madness. A tongue with virginal vowels and imploded plosives.

I was thoroughly lost until the moment when events forced me to my ultimate moment of degradation. It was the night the maestro came up to the attic.

That night was the last one that melia would say the Lord's Prayer before sleeping. Henceforth, she would no longer wish for mom and dad to be well, for her dog to be well with the one white and the one black eye. Those were her prayers as a young child under the care of the green-light lamp, but on that particular night, the small green lamp would burn out and in the wake of that disaster a new bad day would follow.

the rape

In the name of the Father

before she left for school each morning, her dad used to peel an orange for his daughter so that her hands wouldn't smart

and the Son

her home had the smell of oranges

and the Holy Ghost

every time she tasted an orange her palate hurt, then she choked

Amen

all the oranges left by the daughter were eaten by the mother, so that nothing would be wasted in this place called home.

Our Father, who art in Heaven

Across the attic there was a round house where a maestro lived, her father's age. From the attic the bedroom of the round house could be seen. The maestro paid her a visit.
Impressive though of uncommonly small stature.

Hallowed be thy name, thy kingdom come

She was sitting on the low garden wall within which the plants were incarcerated, sipping pomegranate juice when he came up to invite her to his house and tell her all about his music systems. He spoke to her about the ruler, the compass, the two styluses, the three candleholders and the coffin. He had seen the rough gemstone and became obsessed with turning it into a hewn one. She would be the pupil and he the Teacher. Initiation level 9.

thy will be done,

Though shy when it came to invitations of that sort, the next moment she found herself looking at the attic from the round bedroom. It was a two-storey house, the whole of the upper level was one bedroom. It was all glassed in, she went up close and thought that with one more step, she's out in the void, she touched the glass and a circle was imprinted on it that looked like the age of innocence.

Would she follow on the Teacher's path? Uncompromising in her Christian faith, her life under persecution?

It was cold but she'd neglected to put gloves on. Her hands were precious, her fingers ten in number, she wasn't going to grow any taller, her adolescence had reached its date of expiry. Her breath fogged the window pain. It was raining torrentially that night.

on earth as it is in heaven;

Raindrops forcefully crashed and nervously dispersed on the bedroom windowpane. The temple bells were tolling wildly and like the lamb to the slaughter, people were lamenting the collapse of the temple.

They're both mortal, it's power they're after, she thought.

give us this day our daily bread

He had undressed her before he had time to realize that the resistance she was putting up is like an incurable disease against which it's no use fighting. Her chest muscles were lax despite her youthfulness and her nipples were inverted as if a thousand and one pigeons had drawn out the milk and emptied the sacks. She didn't take off her brassiere so that the ideal image of her youthfulness would remain untarnished by his seeing her empty breasts.

and forgive us our trespasses,

For the duration of her molestation, the round bed kept changing shapes. His compass was playing with the nerve endings of her ears, their labyrinth becoming ever more convoluted with every renewed penetration. She had closed her eyes so that she wouldn't hurt and was seeing her dad peeling oranges so that her hands wouldn't smart.

He could be my dad, he is his age, she said in a low voice so the man wouldn't hear.

as we forgive those who trespass against us;

She saw herself as a child peeking through the half-open bedroom door at her dad between her mom's thighs. Life is an open door that won't close. Who'll close the door? Lovemaking can't be taught, I said to myself.

lead us not to temptation,

The maestro was making sounds through his mouth "no one can cometh unto the Father but by me", a rotten eggshell cracking for a small half-dead dove to be born. She remained speechless. The round house, the round bedroom, the round bed, the round age were carving a deaf-mute language onto her palate, a place where the secret could be hidden.

and deliver us from evil;

The following days everything seemed normal, the nights in the attic normal, yet her jagged glances molested from a distance the round house whose windowpanes remained fogged up even on the sunniest days. Her pupils were dilated and she became tearful whenever she heard music. "How did I ever become so sensitive?" The memory of a compass crawling in her path was calling out to her.

Amen.

In the name of

her dad's oranges had been sour

our Lord

her mom had never acknowledged their sourness, waste not what not in this place called home

Jesus Christ

for some strange reason she would not buy oranges for the children she was going to have

Amen.

The members of my body did not follow one from the other, in the manner of a member of the faith who is assailed by doubt; there was a malfunction I was trained to enact by rote, without the slightest spontaneous conviction, with propriety like sour orange and all inner joy cast aside. An amputated atmosphere in a house with no garden, or a garden with no house. How much longer would I have the strength to bear it?

I had left the house, I left the attic, I left the lovers; I stopped running and mom's depression in the form of a black angel never again visited me in my dreams.

architecture

Miltos lowered the book down to the level of his nose and he met melia's eyes. Two egg- shaped bulbs covered by membranous sheaths of brown color. The brown branched out into an underground system of green roots and, instead of black, the pupil was a deep royal blue. Maybe this was the first time that the sensation of an image was stronger than a rational explanation. Miltos' level look, without no subterfuge, was powerful enough to restore attraction to the wounded woman melia was.

"What can I do for you?" he smiled at her.

Closed off in herself like she was used to being, she realized with astonishment that she had hesitantly sat down at the strange man's table. His impact on her was reinforced by his smell. Maybe this was the first time that the sensation of a smell was stronger than a rational explanation. Maybe this was the first time that the flow of the phrase "What-can-I- do-for-you" until all its syllables were uttered, dissolved the fear she felt every time she was verbally assaulted by men who needed to build up their ego.

She didn't quite have something to say to him. She didn't know for what reason precisely she had approached him to start with, apart from the fact that an energy drew her to him and defined the boundaries between them. His slender, sparse form occupied a larger space than the one he physically occupied. His shoulder-length hair was cut in layers, ending in sharp, sword-like points. He was having a double espresso.

The first thing she thought of was asking him what he was reading. It was a book on architecture which analyzed the delineation of private, personal space and the peaceful sense of peace in cohabitation. He shut the book. He was an architect. He concentrated on the deep royal blue of her eyes. They started chatting.

Initially they spoke about the sea and about abandonment. They spoke about the rain and the foundations of houses. They spoke until dawn. It was unorthodox for both to find so many unexpected things to talk about. It was strange that they didn't feel awkward with one another, not even momentarily.

Miltos' silence was not noisy and melia realized that by his side, she would find the calmness she so badly needed in order for her soul to heal. Maybe he was the first person to whom she spoke openly about the strangeness of her existence, given she was without a brain, and he certainly was the first person who pass no comment, even about her crooked foot. He listened to her carefully without melia needing to repeat what she'd said in order for Miltos to believe the unbelievable. What a relief!

Before they parted they promised to meet at the same coffee-shop, same time next day. This habit lasted for about a year.

Miltos loved melia and melia needed Miltos in order to find the thing ahainst which she had transgressed since her childhood. Her freedom. He wasn't going to be an obstacle to her.

Next year Miltos put in the foundations of their joint home where melia gave birth

to Mia.

writer-subject relationship

In this coffee-shop, in this house, in this neighborhood, in this city, in this country, in this world, in this book where everyone uses everyone else, Miltos will be an imaginary exception.

the couple

Ten years had passed since that first meeting of melia with Miltos. Details. Time's true passing cannot be recorded. They were good friends at first. Friendship led them to love, love led them to conflict and next came a marriage. They were both still young.

Frequently and fleetingly, images and moments returned to melia's mind of her parents who had been the simulation of the "couple" deemed to be "happy".

To melia her parents' "couple" was where you find the other by losing yourself and you shine like a bright denture over rotten teeth. She didn't want that to happen to her.

The two people who had so successfully negotiated their incarceration inside the roles of "dad" and "mom", had, in the daughter's absence, unexpectedly ejected their most heartfelt fears outside the family bowl like elderly fish throwing themselves out of the sea, gasping for breath.

Following their separation, melia's dad started getting old and her mom grew even more silent, sinking into her depression.

melia was anxious about what makes a "perfect" couple. Given she'd found in Miltos an unexpectedly likeable partner, might not the two of them be the perfect couple?

A pair of shoes may be of a particular shape and size, but they can be worn by many different feet.

A pair of eyes may belong to the same face but they can have different degrees of myopia.

A pair of earrings may be of the same weight or they may not.

In a dancing couple if one partner picks up new routines and the other doesn't, you change partners.

A pair of trees. There are no pairs of trees.

Since she couldn't locate the "perfect couple" she started to wonder what "a couple" is, looking at her relationship.

Throughout this time "the couple" was experiencing what being married is like. Between melia and Miltos who had been pronounced her husband by law nine years previously, a new language had evolved. It wasn't hers, it wasn't his, it wasn't a common one and it wasn't mine. It was the language of an institution. An institution with restraining terms and latent grammar.

Every night a backwards move and their bodies detonated like silent atomic bombs, as soon as they touched the bed, ordering the silencing of all true desires. Because it was late, because the day had been tiresome, because the roles were demanding, because there was satiation, because there was a running nose.

Every night a backwards move. A move from the spouse role. Her mom always gave her a piece of advice which she hadn't succeeded in keeping herself, "no matter what happens never kick your husband out of bed"; she hadn't advised "no matter what happens, never leave the bed". Like a good daughter she never kicked Miltos out of bed and like a good spouse, she never left the bed. No matter what had happened.

It had been some time that she hadn't seen her mom and dad. She received their news but kept her distance from her family, convinced that the story wouldn't repeat itself.

Every night a backwards move. To maintain a steady output in the spouse role, she used as justification the conviction that the blame does not rest with marriage as an institution, but with marriage as a habit.

Nevertheless, marriage knew better than melia what it was and what it claimed.

Time was its favorite game.

Let us calculate and see how the game of time is played.

Marriage is an adept player, the betrothed are novice players. Marriage is well familiar with terms of time, knows all the winning moves. The slower its opponents are to pick up new learning, the easier the prognosis is of their time. By making the wrong moves they grow short of breathing space and become addicted to an illicit relationship with the death of the relationship. The apprentice couple should know the terms of time before they make a deal to play with marriage, before they find themselves exposed to the opponent, before they start getting angry with their ignorance, before they start to need the game, before they become addicted to winning and losing, before their relationship becomes a ghost that is bidding its time till their collapse.

Every night a backwards move. A move of retreat. It's not the institution of marriage that is to blame, it's addiction.

In nine years of marriage melia and Miltos at least shared the same bed, two meters by two in diameter.

How deeply had premonition been anaesthetized?

there're many other things as well

Every night the autistic motion was magnified of my body which was trying to stay still so I could fall asleep. It was perceptible to the extent that I was thinking about it and, so, I couldn't sleep.

There're a lot of things.

Like the spasms of Miltos who lay by my side for years on end. A peculiar kind of snoring which every once in a while, though not with any specific rhythm, reached a climax as if he was breathing his last. When I nudged him with my hand or foot to make him stop – not because he was so noisy but because it bothered me that a person should behave so out of control in their sleep – then some part of him – not he, himself – assured me that everything is alright. That everyone is in their appointed place.

There are many other things as well.

Like the imperceptible shudder, for many years, of the spider's web in between the metal shanks of the central heating unit, where no implement could reach to rout it out. I lived with a spider as a house pet without having chosen to.

There are many other things as well.

Like the rhythmic ticking of the clock that is born only by means of a battery and can die only by means of a flat battery.

A sound I could hear only when the house was taken over by the complete soundlessness of its residents, an inconceivable thing because people take revenge on themselves by ignoring the meaning of speaking and so they talk without pause, cause or gist.

There are many other things as well.

Like the wooden figure of a Pinocchio, a gift by my grandmother, hanging from the ceiling over our heads – wrong room, this isn't the nursery – whose nose would start getting longer at night, getting under the bedcovers and exploring my nether parts.

There are many other things as well.

Like the clothes in the wardrobe hanging tightly against one another without any breathing space. They kept a diary with memories of their own from moments of mine. Every night they make me remember, they make me forget. Sensations from touches which no detergent could remove.

There are many other things as well.

Like the subjects of the books scattered on every flat surface, living lives every night which no biological mother ever gave them. When events such as births and deaths took place in those lives, I'd suddenly wake up and facing the familiar dark, I would ask Miltos "did you hear that?" "It's nothing, you imagined it" he'd answer.

How had the two of us grown so alienated? What power greater than ourselves was at work to separate us?

There were many other things as well.

One of the many nights I saw myself sitting with arms folded across from me, looking at me puzzled. Sitting next to her, angry and weak, was the small boy, his hair knotty and patent shoes dusty as if he 'd been trekking across sand dunes. I grew scared of the coming storm. Or was it to be cleansing waters that would wash out the habit of the institution of marriage which had spread like sediment all over the truth?

This was a calm angel. He spread out his arms ready to take flight, except he was missing his wings. I got so scared that an instantaneous pain transported me back to the family home, when I was breathing there in the dark. In the wardrobe mirror I saw in our bed, mom in my side and dad in Miltos. Outside the rain had started.

The previous afternoon I had bought a green plant in a white pot. The color suited me and the size, I put it on the dresser, in between the books, next to the wardrobe, near the clock across from the central heating unit, under Pinocchio. They say you shouldn't sleep with a plant in your room because it sucks up your oxygen. Miltos and I went to sleep.

In the morning the plant was dead and I could feel a wind blowing in the house, bringing rain with it. I turned, saw my husband asleep by my side. I lost all control.

Who was this man with whom I had been sharing my life for years?

I couldn't exactly pinpoint the way in which marriage had led me to lose those parts of myself I had rescued by leaving the family home. The family home had grown enormous and had established itself inside the house of my marriage. I had allowed myself to grow inert, although I knew that this failing would usher me into abandonment.

The awareness I had attained all these years had been exclusively through self-recognition. Inside marriage this condition by itself wasn't enough.

Dueling with the acts that had been committed but could not be explained inside the still waters of marriage, I was exposed to fear. My sorrow took on the dimensions of my shadow on the wall and my existence shrank inside the bounds of my body, inside the impossible regime in which I was raising my daughter Mia.

I saw the young boy with the knotted hair and dusty patent shoes waiting for me, his back turned to the front door. My tongue was tied in knots from my past and could not be loosened to speak. I had to go back home. Back to the family home, back to my parents. I needed to untie the knots, to speak. I buried the dead plant at the foot of the garden's red tree and started digging to find the way back into a story that remained unfinished.

death

In the manner of an acute childhood sickness, melia's vision became blurry every time she watched her mom cry. After her return to the family home, she watched death feasting on her mom as if he was a most welcome visitor. She had made a bet with herself that she would manage to get a glimpse of "him", so that she could ask "him" this one question:

"where?"

"where will you take mom so I can come and visit?"

She had lied. She had lied when she'd said she didn't love her.

She got very sick. When she became well, she was told she was never going to be able to see her again.

They never spoke with her dad about mom again. She never did ask him "where".

She realized that, had her dad known where, he would have taken her there on foot, by carriage, by train, by boat, he'd even sew wings on her so she could fly there, one way or another he'd have taken her to see mom. She realized that had her dad known how, he would have made amends years ago. That wasn't his way. The time he spent away from his wife and daughter taught him to observe them without judging them. Through the distance he had loved them more than he had suspected and this was a guileless love because he knew he didn't need them.

After years, melia was seeing her dad grow white and calm, numb in relation to a past which had not been preserved. They were two strangers. This was valid reason for them to wish to become friends. There wasn't going to be a new beginning. There was no new beginning in the family vocabulary.

She had been familiar with her mom's silence but she was feeling nostalgic for her words. She looked for them in the diary left behind as testament by a woman who was no longer alive.

the diary

I miss my Melia.

....

For days now I walk around covered in the stains of the
destruction. The molecules of ash hovering like drugged
insects in the dangerous atmosphere of this neverland, stick
to my skin.
My pores are clogged.

....

I can't think.

....

I should get up and make some coffee, eat an orange.
The night light is out. I can feel the light coming in through
the window shutters.

....

I can feel?

....

I eat. I worry I might choke on a fishbone.

Afterwards, a chocolate egg.

....

I have a very slight fever.

The man has been gone from the house for years. I am truly alone. The woman at the basement is making things ready. She is putting to order every incompetence of mine. I can hear the sound of the washing machine from the depths of the basement.
The dog's in the yard. He is looking at me.

I am very angry.
I am an ill-willed, preliminary draft of the person I could have been.

I go down to the basement, use the round entrance of the washing machine to get inside that dark hole and close the door made of unbreakable glass, suitable for very high temperatures.

....

The weather is nice outside. The house is always cold. The sun never gets to it.

....

I miss my Melia.

....

I am now curled inside the black hole like a puzzled foetus.

....

Should take my pills. Not to forget. Won't forget to take my pills. How could I possible forget to take my pills. I never forget to take my pills. Mustn't forget to take my pills.

....

Third day that the dog is in the same spot. If he could speak, would words speak for him? Except he can't. He's a dog.

....

With the door closed, space is tight with no air supply, all choked up in silent darkness. I feel against my back two metal cylinders, drum-shaped. In the silent darkness, with a terrifying small sound, like a thud, the cylinders start revolving in opposite directions. With every forward and backward revolution, soapy water is sloshed around.

....

I see the woman in the balcony next door. I'm thinking that all these years we've been neighbors we haven't exchanged a single word, no good morning, no goodnight.

She sees me and smiles at me for the first time.

....

I relax and surrender to the soapy water and I begin, in the foetal position with my arms protecting my head, to revolve with an unnatural rage, washing off my anger and cleaning the ash from my body.

....

I miss my Melia.

...I smile back at her. She's dyed her hair bright red to disguise the white hairs. Now that they're out of sight, her hair shines. My eyes are clear today.

....

I feel like a fish that's escaped the fishing hook by sticking close to a rock and has been granted the freedom to swim away and breathe in deep clear waters.

....

I open the balcony door to let in some air and see the dog looking at me. He is staring at me in despair as if he's perceived something that I cannot. He hasn't shifted his position. He is lying exactly at the spot I left him yesterday.

He hasn't had any food. I should go out and pet him. Should I feed him some orange?

....

The coffee's boiled over, on top of everything. It's stuck to the pot like a second skin. I try to scrape it off with a knife, then I use my nails. My nails are blackened.

....

I sit in the kitchen rocking chair and watch the dog looking at me. I don't know what comes over me and I start sobbing. As I try to clean my blackened nails by chewing them and spitting out the black bits, I see that the dog is wallowing in all the things he's let go of out of his anus, his urethra and his mouth.

....

I am upset, virtually terrified. I watch him open up a black hole to drool in and, after he covers it up, he looks up at me again and again and again. He does that three times and it taxes him so much that his body sticks to his bones, his eyes glued to mine.

....

He keeps at it for several minutes. I don't keep the time, but it doesn't seem that long.

....

When he gives up the effort, I get up, go down to the yard and take the dog in my

arms. I've never in my life held a dead body, it isn't something I know anything about. But so what?

....

I sit with my dead dog in my arms and I wait. But so what?

....

Sadness is blacker than my nails. But so what?

....

I am waiting for the man to return and take charge of the situation. It doesn't cross my mind that the man has been gone for years. Nor that, though I cry at every opportunity, I am unable to cry over death.

....

I miss my Melia.

....

I sit in the kitchen rocking chair with my dead in my arms. Only dead did the dog come inside the house. He liked living in the yard, frequented by the roots of the red tree, dug holes there to hide his bones.

....

Tomorrow the housekeeper will arrive and find me in the same position. She will gently take the dead out of my arms. I won't ask her where she's going. Where can she possibly go cradling a corpse?

....

I eat an orange and go to bed.

....

I miss my Melia.

....

My only thought is that Holy Week starts tomorrow.

....

I go into a long sleep. I have a nightmare where a javelin flies out of an orange as I'm eating it and tears out my eyes, crushing the lids and the lenses. Not a drop of blood in sight. From inside the orange a voice whispers "no matter how far you manage to get, it'll always be the same. No matter under which tap you wash, the ashes will remain".
Completely blinded, I watch my mother warm some milk.

As she turns and sees me, she grabs me by the hair and kisses me on the lips. "What's the matter, you look like you've seen a ghost" she says.

"No, I just had nightmare."

"Turn the tap on and let the water wash away the bad dream", she says.

....

I run out to the yard and hide in the roots of the red tree, where the dog is buried in the grave dug by the housekeeper. Inside the hole she dug, she found a bunch of bones.

....

I live in the same spot for years, unmoving.

....

As soon as I get back home I'll run the bath and get back in the waters out of which I emerged....

....

Goodbye my daughter.

the end

The time was late and tiredness had taken its toll on the body's stamina. melia had fallen asleep beside me and was crying softly in her sleep over the dead dog of her childhood.

I read the rest of her mom's diary and it was only too familiar. I knew all about loss.

I'd experienced it when I was young with my Father's loss. It had made me arrogant and ambitious, thinking I could change the story by writing it down and furnishing a different ending.

During the last years of her life, melia's mom was very sick. She recognized the time was drawing near for her question to be answered which she hadn't put to anyone. She was grown enough to have accepted the fact that it would not be possible to see "him". And that the blame didn't lie with her sorrowful sight but with his permanent absence, despite the fact that "he" is more present than anyone else.

melia put her mother in a clinic for people with Alzheimer's and lived the loss of her mom's memory for an entire winter. Mom and melia remained connected with an umbilical cord that was severed after her death.

the illness

Her illness was like a live ghost which had inhabited mom.
The sound she made had a dark- colored tone, was full of
snot at the bottom of the throat. The illness had anchored
there as well. Her eyes dry, like a statue staring at a place
beyond vision. As if opening her arms for the void to
enthrone itself there. The half-opened lips attempted sounds.
They failed.

Her image got out of the chair which supported
her weight and seemed to open the window with the
grey curtains with the white lace at the corners, which
overshadowed the room. The sky was black, night and day
for a whole year.

The white nightgown with the yellow lace trimming and
her name embroidered on the left hand side, touching her
heart, had grown into a second skin. I am sure she hated it.
She couldn't wash herself. Whenever melia tried to bathe
her, she stopped her.

There was nothing she could do for her. It was
already too late.

It was a rule in this place that you should wear your
name on your person so you could be recognized. Her

mom knew that and she wouldn't let melia take off the white nightgown with her name over her heart.

Illness had visited and her mom entrusted herself to it, as if it had been a long awaited visitor.

Every day she grabbed a marker and forcefully drew a spiral, a new black hole, in her diary. A bottomless well whose end only she could reach.

She refused to eat or drink, she refused to sleep.

She sat battle-ready in the rocking chair, with perfect ease, and stared at the window with the gray curtains. Which was shut.

By order of the management.

except, how could she possibly kill herself when she didn't even have memories? how could she possibly kill herself when she had been declared incompetent?

and why ever should she?

The night she found her mother's pale body floating weightless, without a trace of life, in the bathtub of the institution, she hadn't cried. A horrible feeling of joy and sadness interchangeably produced a sense of relief. She knew one thing. She felt free. Like an eagle with wounded wings flying out of its cage.

She didn't cry the next night either. She couldn't remember herself crying. She had convinced herself of the love due by a child to its parents, yet she wasn't able to cry over their loss.

Her mom had been taking pills for many years. And when mom was no longer alive, her dad collapsed. A strange thing it was that when her dog died, her mom didn't cry and when her mom died, her dad didn't cry. People within a family take up strange habits.

There were moments when melia recalled her mom alive. Then, it was as if she burrowed in mom's arms and all her worries disappeared. As if she was young again, like waking up after a good eight-hour sleep and the day is starting with the smell of mom's cologne and of the fresh lilies in the vase in front of the icon of the Virgin Mary.

melia had no cologne and no vase of lilies.

She had a diary with black holes. The same number as her mother's days.

The last time she looked her daughter in the eye, her gaze was so similar to her full holes, so full of love that can't be put to words or described, so suspended, like the roots of a tree planted in midair, so very much her own, like the mosquito net of her childhood above her pillow, reminiscent of malaria or fever or a shallow plane with wheat thinly sprouting in white fields and shallow lakes, thinly and of its own accord, don't you worry about me mom, you, too, existed thinly, for a moment between being born and dying, broken by what life?, like a branch that didn't intertwine with any other branch, broken, you fell to the ground and impatiently waited for your funeral rites. Into a small hole deep in the earth, a small grave for you, beloved stapling.

the anger

She was frantically looking for her pencil erasers. She couldn't bear to burn her mom's diary. She knew she wouldn't change anything in the story already committed to paper. She wanted to erase some parts. To erase parts of her mom and rewrite them from the beginning as if everything was different, the way she had imagined it, the way she'd wished it, so that it wouldn't hurt her.

She couldn't find her pencil erasers. She was looking frantically but couldn't find them. She was angry, the way she had been angry in the past when trying to understand why dad and mom always called her pretty, never clever. It was obvious and you could tell she was pretty, it was obvious and you couldn't tell she was clever. It was obvious and you could tell she was obedient, it was obvious and you couldn't tell that she would stay angry for a long time. Why was there no will for – any of – the things you couldn't tell?

Because melia knew about herself what her parents, teachers and the whole wide world had been persuaded must be ignored. melia's brain did not lodge in her skull, she had no home, she had no teacher, she had never been to school. Nobody counted on the existence of her brain with the exception of her crooked leg.

In her isolation as a child, melia longed for the grownups to understand her, while the grownups wondered about this miracle, about its purpose. melia was losing touch with them. What circumstance was there in which they might believe in what was not obvious, in what they had not seen nor would ever see.

melia was angry for many years that passed as quickly as heavenly bodies falling from the sky. You are told "there's a falling star, make a wish", but you never have time to see it and the wish never comes true.

When melia grew up, she started trying to understand when it was that she started being so angry. She recalled the grownups' lack of will, their paucity of will. melia's lack of a brain had taken away her mom's voice, had caused her dad's perfect absence, had prompted people to disbelieve the fact of her existence. She had to turn the anger which hurt her into a virtue. If only a single person could be found who understood her.

From the other side of the house, she heard her daughter Mia telling off the dog. It had been a little over a year that melia had been away from her home, a little over a year since Mia had seen her mother and, since her return, Mia was stuck to her like a patch that sucks out the pain.

The dog had eaten the pencil erasers and a baby pigeon that was just attempting its first flight. Mia was angry with the dog.

melia had confessed to Miltos that she loved their months-old, adopted dog and also that she was tired of picking up its droppings from the garden. She'd asked her husband to teach the dog to defecate outside the house.

She had merely asked him to walk the dog. Miltos promised he would. He was the only person who kept his promises. melia believed. It is enough.

the glass

The years passed, time is defined by the seasons and the seasons changed their outer aspect, though not their etymology in the dictionary.

Mia was growing up observing her mother and asking her – why, every time a person dies, is another person born? - melia made no answer, she only autistically swept the floors, folded clothes in drawers and set out the table with linen on Sundays.

Miltos caressed his wife with his eyes and answered his daughter – unsolvable riddles.

melia had been afraid of birth, as if it was old age. She believed that even with need

of riddles, she'd have to die one day anyway. Her brain belonged to no one, even though that too, was questionable.

What subject narrates its story?

The book I had been writing, with melia's story, was missing pages, it was shrinking in size, the more so as her mind was turning into a hook looking for a breadcrumb to latch onto.

She would not go mad. From a young age her height had served her size well. It is enough.

The dog was no longer a puppy and from the moment Miltos could trust him without a leash, he was walked by melia and Mia, though on that particular day, night seemed to have descended more swiftly than usual. The place looked different because spring was passionately in evidence. The dry grassland with the large empty patches had been transformed into a forest of long, flower-bearing stems; their leaves caressed the two women's bodies and spikelets got into their skin, inflicting small wound. The unexpected assaults by thorns and toxic weeds caused them to itch and break out in red patches.

In the forest of long-stemmed flowers running along the wall of melia's and Miltos' property, there was a narrow path that went some distance. Mia led and melia followed. The dog was gone, chasing a swarm of bees.

melia was terrified, though of what, the night forest and the unknown in the darkness or the dog who, though he heard his name being called, didn't deign to come back, playing a silly power game like that of her father? Mia felt no fear, melia was shaking all over, until the point where the forest started giving way and mother and daughter were able to see out to the sea. This was the first time they'd crossed the forest, gone such a great distance from the house. How many hours did it take? No walk in the past had taken them quite this far. How was it possible for the sea to be so near and them not know it? There was a big ship waiting on the shore. It looked abandoned but intact.

It shone inside the darkness like a piece of glass and it reflected three female bodies.

In the glass melia herself, her daughter, her mother.

after death

The reflection was so strong that I got dizzy, I lay back a bit and there, by the sea, I fell asleep for a short while. I had a dream.

I see

my mom in a lake

I see

her mind moistened by the green waters. She has red hair and she's sitting in front of me at the edge of the lake with her bare toes in the water

I see

that I don't have dad's toes, I have mom's

I see

only the back of her and a swan, whose wings are also oars.

A bird-fish, I think to myself.

There are some monstrous trees rooted at the bottom of the lake whose leaves throw a possessive shadow. I stare intently at the back of the red-haired woman in front of me. She gets up and, taking slow steps, she sinks into the water without even turning to look at me.

I follow her.

"I am coming" is the last word I utter and for some reason, though I should repeat it, for some reason, I don't.

I woke up tired.

"Come", Mia said, "come with me now". I pulled the girl by the hand and told her it's still early.

We didn't speak about the night in the forest, we didn't speak about the sea we discovered that night or any other night. The dog had gone back to the house before the two of us. He was standing outside the rail fence waiting. His breath was salty.

the housekeeper

The housekeeper dusted the glass case which contained the bridal gown, the wedding wreaths, the umbrella and sandals which melia wore at her wedding, the ecclesiastical psalms and the initialed broach which Miltos wore on his lapel, a wedding gift from her mom. After the death of his wife, melia's dad had secluded himself and lived without contact with his daughter's family. Mia never knew him as melia had, never spent time with him.

The housekeeper dusted the diary of melia's mom, Mia's grandmother, which was on the bedside table on melia's side of the bed. Every time the housekeeper found Mia lying in her mother's bed, she took her in her arms and softly spoke to her about her mother.

That she had been strong, that she hadn't been afraid to be different, she hadn't been afraid of the Other, she hadn't been afraid of emptiness, she hadn't been afraid of the desert, she hadn't been afraid to leave.

That she took the path to the sea where the ship had been waiting, abandoned but intact.

That she went up to it turning her back to the forest and, behind the forest, to the family home and, behind the family home, to her life.

That she caressed her crooked leg feeling the protective touch of Miltos' eyes, until the ship was no more than an infinitely small dot in time.

That, at that moment, she was whispering her first declaration of faith in herself, who was becoming "whole" on that day, more than on any day before or after.

That someday the daughter would come to understand her mother, even if she could not forgive her.

That no one ever saw her again. That she's not even a memory.

the escape

The groove was still in the bed where melia had fallen asleep the last time we met, exhausted by her confession.

I turned my palm up and looked at the life line, melia had a visible form and shape, her face was familiar to me, her eyes were a royal blue color and her skin was rough, her strong voice that some time ago had whispered "come with me now" had grown so weak I could barely hear it. I felt quiet and I felt happy. She had dwelt in her own country. I closed my palm and touched her for a few minutes on the chest, over the heart.

As far as the end of her story goes, I didn't change it, I didn't even write it. I had had myself a snack food and then I had gone out of the small apartment for a walk. A walk, that's all I wanted, just a walk.

prophecy

Many years back, I don't recall how many, I started looking for the x. of my childhood. I don't know what particular reason made me want to meet him. In truth, I was certain that x. hadn't survived that cold winter and the hot summer. As I mentioned at the beginning, x. was a weak child. I could find no trace of him anywhere and so, one day, I stopped looking for him and made do with his one and only image that was imprinted in my memory. The deep parting in his thick hair that divided his head in two, the creation of his widowed mother. Without realizing it, I was covering alongside him, my own feminine path on my own male child's head. A path with many obstacles that fortified me greatly. This was the time when I started reading. This was the time when I stopped being afraid of death.

The story of the book's writing

On July 9 I was born.

Nine characters I created. I discovered this after I had completed the book.

The true identities of my characters are invented because the people who live inside their ID papers have escaped, relinquishing personal responsibility for their true identity. My own ID documents are blank. There is nothing there. I created a true document by taking responsibility for writing a book. I thus accepted and forgave myself, allowed myself to be reborn and to live. Writing the book helped me understand that when we are little, we become creators of the imagination in order to survive and when we grow up, we become creators of our reality in order to live. I didn't know this at the beginning.

The true Maria is the writer.
The invented Maria is Chris.
Maria is melia.

melia is free to come and go every time the book is opened.

Maria who created in silence, Maria who allowed the fragments to become "one whole". Maria who invented herself in order to exist.

The life line is an alphabet etched in my palm. An alphabet of invention of people who are not me. That is my past. My palm now is as smooth as glass. I exist present in the now.

In the writing of the story I was absent, hidden behind Chris who is hiding behind x. who is being written by Chris in order for melia to appear. melia who is present in her absence insofar as she is invented. Chris invented the story of the dead Siamese sister who was cut off from him after birth.

Could Chris possibly carry inside one of his organs the brain of melia, as his dead invented sister, giving her back the life she didn't live?

Could Chris' lungs be melia?

Chris breathes and his lungs are thinking. Chris needs melia in order to think free of guilt and fearless, because the life line, the hair parting and, finally, language always lead back to the one, the greatest fear of all.

The writing of the book lasted three years. Not for a story to be told, not for a book to be written. Every year a new subject turned up. melia was the one to visit me first since she always existed in me; after a year melia turned up with x. Out of observing the relationship of those two, Chris came into being. Not the other way around.

Three years ago, the story of my own mythography began (I didn't then know the content) and I invented myself in order to write it. Because nothing out of all the things written was as real as facing the final knowledge which I derived from them, the fact that in being present I am absent and in being absent I am present, always.

That nobody ever "sees" me.

That I "am" not even a memory.

And one other thing, even more important now that it's done, I have learned

that

nothing is ever "difficult".

About the Author

 **Maria Olon Tsaroucha** is a visionary thought leader, internationally acclaimed actor, director, educator, and author of the Amazon bestseller *SUPRACONSCIOUS: The Genius Within You*. As the founder of the *Supraconscious You* Breakthrough, she has spent over two decades pioneering a humanistic, artistic, and scientific approach to consciousness, identity, and personal evolution.

Maria's work is a unique blend of ancient ethics, modern neuroscience, quantum physics, and the art of method acting. This distinctive approach allows her to delve into the profound question of *'Who Am I and How I Live as my Highest Self.'*

From global stages like TEDx to humanitarian missions and transformative workshops across continents, Maria's work has resonated with a diverse range of people. She is known for igniting profound shifts in scientists, artists, educators, visionaries, and seekers alike.

At the remarkable age of thirteen, Maria penned her first book, a feat that earned her the title of the youngest Greek author ever.

"Your life is not your résumé. It is your revelation."
— *Maria Olon Tsaroucha*

More books by Maria Olon Tsaroucha:
*Embark on transformative journeys and discover profound wisdom within Maria Olon Tsaroucha's works. Visit her Amazon Author Page to explore **more of her** books, where she continues to inspire with stories of consciousness, self-discovery, and the power of the human spirit.*